THE PARROT SONG

Édouard Manceau

Tate Publishing

One, two, three . . .
Repeat after me!

There once was a little cloud . . .

There once was a little cloud!

It rained every colour . . .

It rained every colour!

Red, yellow, green and blue . . .

Red, yellow, green and blue!

So the flowers grew and grew . . .

So the flowers grew and grew!

Ready for us to pick a few . . .

Ready for us to pick a few!

And bring them all the way
to you . . .

And bring them all the way
to you!

Knock, knock, knock. May I come in?

Knock, knock, knock. May I come in?

Here's a gift for my friend, Tim . . .

Here's a gift for my friend, Tim . . .

He gave to me a box of blue . . .

He gave to me a box of blue!

And three cheeky parrots popped up. Peekaboo . . .

And three cheeky parrots popped up. Peekaboo!

They are the ones who taught me how . . .

They are the ones who taught me how!

To sing the parrot song . . .

LET'S
ALL SING
TOGETHER NOW!

First published in English in 2017 by order of the Tate Trustees by Tate Publishing, a division
of Tate Enterprises Ltd, Millbank, London, SW1P 4RG
www.tate.org.uk/publishing
First published in French as 'La Comptine Des Perroquets'
© 2016, Albin Michel Jeunesse, Paris – www.albin-michel.fr
Translated by Annie Eaton. © 2017 Tate Enterprises Ltd
A catalogue record for this book is available from the British Library
ISBN 978 1 84976 497 1

Distributed in the United States and Canada by ABRAMS, New York
Library of Congress Control Number applied for

Printed and bound in China by Toppan Leefung